THE
NGUYEN KIDS

The Journey of the
ANCESTORS'GIFTS

written by
Linda Trinh

illustrated by
Clayton Nguyen

annick
press
toronto · berkeley

Cover art by Clayton Nguyen, designed by Clayton Nguyen and Sam Tse
Interior designed by Sam Tse
Cover and interior based on the series design by Paul Covello
Edited by Katie Hearn and Jieun Lee
Copy edited by Eleanor Gasparik
Proofread by Mary Ann Blair

Annick Press Ltd.

We acknowledge the support of the Canada Council for the
Arts and the Ontario Arts Council, and the participation of the
Government of Canada/la participation du gouvernement du Canada
for our publishing activities.

Image Credits: Page 108, © PrimeMockup/Adobe Stock; Page 109, © Andrii
Zastrozhnov/Adobe Stock; Pages 110-111, © Doraemon/Adobe Stock

Library and Archives Canada Cataloguing in Publication

Title: The journey of the ancestors' gifts / written by Linda Trinh ; illustrated by Clayton Nguyen.
Names: Trinh, Linda, author. | Nguyen, Clayton, illustrator.
Series: Trinh, Linda. Nguyen kids.
Description: Series statement: The Nguyen kids
Identifiers: Canadiana (print) 20230169333 | Canadiana (ebook) 20230169341 |
ISBN 9781773218120 (hardcover) | ISBN 9781773218137 (softcover) |
ISBN 9781773218151 (PDF) | ISBN 9781773218144 (HTML)
Classification: LCC PS8639.R575 J68 2023 | DDC jC813/.6—dc23

Published in the U.S.A. by Annick Press (U.S.) Ltd.
Distributed in Canada by University of Toronto Press.
Distributed in the U.S.A. by Publishers Group West.

Printed in Canada

annickpress.com
lindaytrinh.com
claytonnguyen.art

Also available as an e-book. Please visit annickpress.com/ebooks for more details.

For my family in Vietnam—
let's keep our stories alive.
—L.T.

For my family in Vietnam
and abroad.
—C.N.

TABLE OF CONTENTS

CHAPTER 1: ANNE
Grandma Nội's House

"This is amazing," I whisper, standing in front of the house Grandma Nội grew up in. I close my eyes to enjoy the moment.

"Move, Miss Perfect!" Liz pushes past me. The house is tall and narrow and painted light green. I am super excited to learn what Grandma Nội's life was like here in Vietnam. That may help me learn

about where my parents came from and where I come from.

An older woman, with long, straight hair, waves us inside.

Dad hurries to the door, a suitcase in each hand. "Chào Chị Ba," he says as he greets the woman.

They speak in Vietnamese and hug and laugh. I'm glad she seems nice.

My body tingles with excitement. But once I'm inside the house, I feel a heaviness on my shoulders. It's a bit spooky.

Jay holds Mom's hand as they come inside last. "I don't want you or Dad to go," he whispers to Mom.

I try to help. "Jay, it's only for five days. We will have fun!"

Dad puts his hands on Jay's shoulders. "We'll get you settled first. Okay, Jaco—buddy."

He was going to say Jacob. Jay asked us to stop calling him that a few months ago. I think it is harder for Dad and Mom to make the change than it is for me. They are older.

"Hello, Chị Ba," Mom says, and then adds, "Liz, Anne, Jay," as she points to each of us.

"Kids, this is your auntie, Cô Ba," Dad says.

Jay and I wave hello.

Liz goes over and hugs our auntie like Dad did.

Jay wipes his eyes. "Why can't we all be together?"

"Mom and Dad want a break. Don't be such a baby!" Liz says, still holding auntie's hand.

"I'm not a baby!" Jay snaps back.

"Liz. Not helpful," I say firmly but gently. It is my job as the oldest sibling to take care of them both. I adjust my glasses, standing a bit straighter. I take my job very seriously.

Liz pauses but then pulls me away, "Explore time!"

She cannot sit still for long.

I touch my jade bangle around my wrist, Grandma Nội's gift to me. She died three years ago. Dad and Mom say we Vietnamese believe the spirits of our family, our ancestors, stay with us after they pass away. We pray to them, and they bring us luck. I believe it.

Grandma Nội's house is so different from

our house in Winnipeg. Walking deeper into it, I imagine when she lived here, over 60 years ago. Past the living room and the stairs is an area open to the sky. Wow. What happens when it rains?

The house may be skinny, but it goes back forever! Moving through the kitchen, I imagine Grandma Nội making chả giò and bánh xèo the way she showed me. Liz races up the flight of stairs two at a time as I climb step by step, not wanting to rush. There are two more levels of rooms and then, the best part, an open rooftop area on the fourth floor. The house is cool, but there's something about it . . . I can't shake the feeling I had when I first walked in, like I'm carrying an invisible backpack.

Heading back downstairs, I notice a closed door on the second floor. Super strange! It's the only closed door in the whole house. What could be in there? Makes me so curious!

My first trip to Vietnam has been fun, touring around the big city on the back of a motorbike and eating street food, and it's been great to get away from all the school and ballet drama back home. I look around and I just know this will be the best part of the whole trip!

I break into a smile. This is going to be super-exciting week—finding out all the secrets of the house!

CHAPTER 2: LIZ
This Is the Life!

I leap into a bedroom on the third floor. Dad already put our bags in here. Anne follows.

I touch my pearl earrings, Grandma Nội's gift to me. Suddenly, an icy-cold feeling shoots down my back. Weird! I shiver a bit but shake it off.

"Cousin Hanh said Grandma Nội shared this room with her sister," I say to Miss Perfect.

There are two mattresses on the floor, a desk, and a dresser. Did Grandma Nội sleep here, giggling with her sister, like me and Anne do?

Anne's looking out a window. "Grandma told me once she and her sister Chị Tư used to ride their bikes up and down the lane, wearing their áo dài tunics. This must be the lane," Anne says.

"And our auntie downstairs, that's Grandma's sister's daughter?" I ask. I know Dad told us, but it's sooooo confusing.

"Yes. Cô Ba is Dad's cousin. Her mom lived in this house and now she does," Anne says and opens her suitcase. She starts to unpack her perfectly rolled clothes and neatly organized books. Boring!

I drop down onto one of the mattresses. "Aah. This is the life!" I roll over on my stomach, my fave position. "Can we get the Wi-Fi password? Messaging to do!" I got the contact info from some of our second cousins that I met last week. We went to a beach resort together. They can practice English. And I can practice Vietnamese. You can never have too many friends.

"I'll ask Dad for it," Anne replies.

I nod. My sister is good to have around . . . sometimes.

"You should unpack."

Ugh, Miss Perfect is also soooo bossy. She's 12 and going into grade seven. That's only two years older than me.

I jump up. I take out my friendship-bracelet-making kit and put it on the dresser. I made a ton of bracelets for family when we were at the beach resort, and I can't wait to make more. Family. Fun. Feeling like I belong. I love making these bracelets!

"Okay, done unpacking! Hey, let's look around outside."

Anne laughs. "Take Jay. I'll go see what Mom and Dad need before they leave."

Jay and I walk around the neighborhood. It took us an hour to get to this town from Ho Chi Minh City where we spent our first week in Vietnam.

Dusty roads. Bikes and motorbikes everywhere. Are there no traffic lights? Horns honking. People chattering and laughing. Dogs barking. So much going on.

"Jay, we're good. Miss Perfect is annoying, but she'll do all the hard stuff for us." I put my arm across his shoulders.

We walk a few blocks to the park Cô Ba told us about. There's a metal play structure at one end and a big green field.

"I miss Grandpa Nội," Jay says.

I nod. I have to remember he is the baby of the family. He's only turning nine next month and going into grade four.

"Me too. And Auntie Hai, Hanh, and Hao! But

you and me can hang out. Make new friends. Have fun!" I say.

He nods, but his face is still tense.

I see four kids about our age playing soccer in the field. I wave to them. No one waves back. Huh!

Possibly they didn't see me.

Okay, so I have things to do this week. Cheer-Up-Jay Plan. And Make-New-Friends-in-Town Plan.

Let the adventure begin!

CHAPTER 3: JAY

Not Like Being in Mexico

I was like a hungry goat when Liz and I got back from the park. Now the soup we ate for dinner feels like bubbles in my stomach. I breathe in and out as Mom and Dad say goodbye. I feel so sad, like a cat in the rain. "So you'll video chat every day, Dad?"

I look down at the painted fan in my hands. It was my gift from Grandma Nội after she passed away. The twelve animals of the Vietnamese zodiac are painted on it. Rat, Buffalo, Tiger, Cat, Dragon, Snake, Horse, Goat, Monkey, Rooster, Dog, and Pig. I was born in the year of the horse. Holding the fan helps me stay calm.

Dad kneels in front of me. "Every day."

Anne hugs me from behind. "I'll take care of them. Enjoy Ha Long Bay!"

I lean into her. "Why can't we go too?" I ask. I hate not getting what I want!

"It's for their wedding anniversary—yuck!" Liz says, hopping over the couch to get to us.

Mom sighs. "Jay, it's Friday, and we'll be back on Wednesday. After that, we'll spend a few more days in the city. Then we fly home."

"Try to have fun. Your first time in Vietnam. Your homeland." Dad smiles, and I force myself to smile back.

It may be your homeland, but it's not mine.

"And Monday, the family is taking you all on a day trip to the mountain," Mom reminds us.

"Be good for Cô Ba. We love you," Dad says.

Mom and Dad kiss us and hug us, and then they disappear into the taxi.

Cô Ba hugs us all, which I don't know if I like. I don't know Cô Ba—she's a stranger. Mom and Dad left us with a stranger.

"Jay . . . sad?"

I'm video chatting with Grandpa Nội, but it's so glitchy. Grrrr . . . another reason I don't like it here.

"Grandpa, I can't hear you or see you," I say. Then the call fails.

After that, I can't sleep. I'm a tiger, pacing around the room. Why can't I share the room with Anne and Liz on the other side of the stairs? Because they're girls?

There is no J sound in Vietnamese, so everyone just calls me bé—baby. I hate it! Anne is Anh and Liz is Lan in Vietnamese, but who am I? Here . . . people look at me and expect things . . . for me to know the language . . . to act a certain way . . . I don't know how to be ME here.

I wish Grandpa Nội was here. He would understand.

Mom and Dad said this summer vacation would be fun, like when we go to Mexico. This is NOT like being in Mexico. When we're there, we build sandcastles, and we don't make our beds, and we eat ice cream all day. Now we're at Grandma Nội's house, and it doesn't *feel* right. There's a snowstorm in my mind, making it hard to think.

I breathe in and out. Just five sleeps until Mom and Dad rescue me. I don't feel like a happy horse, free to gallop around an open field. This week will suck!

CHAPTER 4: ANNE
Something Is Weird

The morning after Mom and Dad leave, Cô Ba goes to the market. Liz and Jay are still sleeping so I look around the house. As I walk through the kitchen, I imagine Grandma Nội cooking with her sister, Cô Ba's mom. Does Cô Ba like living in the house her mom lived in?

Going upstairs, I notice again the room on

the second floor with a closed door. I touch the doorknob. I just have to see what's inside! Like yesterday, I get this strange feeling of heaviness. I think whatever is weighing on me is trying to get my attention . . . make me pay attention to this room.

I open the door, super curious now. Along one wall, there's an altar with candles and an incense holder. We have an altar like this at home. I peek in a little further. And like at home, there is a picture of Grandma Nội on this altar. There are other pictures too, maybe my great-grandparents and other family who have passed away.

Seeing Grandma Nội's picture, I play with the jade bangle on my arm. I wait for the rushing wind, like at home, to know she's around. Nothing. *Where are you, Grandma?*

I tiptoe into the middle of the room, closer to a wooden table with four chairs.

"Anne." Cô Ba is in the doorway. I did not hear her coming, and she does not seem happy.

"Bà Nội?" I say, pointing at the picture on the altar, using the Vietnamese word for grandmother.

She nods but doesn't enter the room.

I start to feel tears in my eyes. Being in this house makes me think of Grandma Nội. I want to feel closer to her. I pick up an incense stick to light.

Cô Ba steps back. "No." Her voice is sad.

"Why?" I ask as I put down the incense.

"No work," she replies.

The incense doesn't work? That seems really . . .

"Anne, where are you?"

Liz yelling from upstairs cuts in on my thoughts.

"Down here," I yell back, still looking at Cô Ba.

Both Jay and Liz come down to the second floor, still in their pajamas.

"Sleepyheads!" I say.

"Is that Grandma Nội?" Jay asks, pointing to grandma's picture on the altar. "Dusty."

I always say Jay pays attention. Only after he says that do I notice how forgotten everything in this room seems. There's no fresh fruit on the altar, like we have at home. The light bulbs in the fake candles are all burnt out.

"Cô Ba, why doesn't lighting incense and praying work here?" I ask.

She shakes her head. "No phước."

"Phước is luck," Liz tells us.

"Dad tells us the ancestors give us luck and help," Jay says.

"Bà Nội đi Canada. Về Việt Nam, không về nhà," Cô Ba says, pointing all around.

"Grandma went to Canada. She comes back to Vietnam, she doesn't come back to the house," Liz translates.

I didn't know that Grandma never came back to the house. She and Grandpa Nội went back to Vietnam many times. I guess they stayed in the city, not here.

"Nhà quên." Cô Ba points to Grandma's picture. "Bà Nội không thể về nhà," Cô Ba adds.

"The house forgot. Now Grandma can't come back," Liz translates.

"Like her spirit can't come back now?" I ask.

"So then no ancestors can give us luck?" Jay asks.

Before we can find out more, the phone rings and Cô Ba heads downstairs.

"This is sooo weird," Liz comments.

"This house is weird," Jay says, a little fear in his voice.

I look at both of them and agree. Something is weird here. I wipe away some dust from Grandma Nội's picture.

I feel a bit of panic as my hands start to sweat. I touch my bangle. Even though I want to tell Liz and Jay I don't sense Grandma here, they shouldn't have to worry. I am the oldest so I should take care of them. But it is a lonely job.

CHAPTER 5: LIZ

Just Scream

It's after lunch, and I need to move. Go. Do. "This is boring. To the park?" I ask.

Miss Perfect's forehead is wrinkly. That happens when she thinks she has to be Miss Responsible-for-Everything.

"Just for a bit. We need to help with dinner," Miss Perfect says and closes the photo album she was looking at.

Jay is sitting outside across the street. He's sketching the front of the house. I wave him back inside.

"Cô Ba, can we go out?" I yell as I run up the stairs. I find her standing outside the ancestors' room.

"Yes." She's wiping her face.

Has she been crying? Does she miss the ancestors giving us luck? I don't know what to say so I just hug her.

She hugs me back, and we walk downstairs where she waves the three of us on our way. "Go."

As I skip down the street, I wish Rohan, Best Friend Ever, was here.

Four kids are playing soccer. I run over.

"Hi. I'm Liz. Can we play?" I pretend to kick the ball.

They all stop playing. They look at me and Jay and Anne.

"I'm Anne, and he's Jay," my sister says beside me.

"Em trai or em gái?" someone whispers, pointing at Jay.

Rude!

Jay looks down. I stand in front of him, shielding him. I'm sooo glad he doesn't know those words in Vietnamese.

"Yes. Play," one girl says.

"No." A boy, tall with wide shoulders and short hair, comes up to me. "Việt Kiều?"

"Sorry?" I say. I don't know what that means.

"Speak Vietnamese?" He crosses his arms, frowning.

"A little. English?" Anne asks in a light voice.

The tall Not-Happy Guy speaks quickly in Vietnamese. I don't catch any of it. All the kids laugh. Again, rude!

My ears start to feel hot.

"Vinh!" the girl says to Not-Happy Guy, shaking her head. She smiles at us. "Hi. I'm Kim."

"You not from here," says another kid, who is shorter and wearing a red T-shirt.

Jay backs up even further.

"Our grandma, our Bà Nội, grew up in the green house over there." Anne points down the street.

Kim's eyes go wide. "Oh, you live in one of *those* houses."

"What do you mean?" Anne asks.

"Your house is cursed," Kim replies.

"What?" I say, thinking about how I got the chills yesterday at the house.

"Your grandma left and never visited the house again. When that happens, the house doesn't welcome any ancestor spirits back. Cursed."

"That's what Cô Ba was trying to say," The Baby whispers.

"Dad would have told us this," I say.

Kim shakes her head. "Việt Kiều don't know. Or they don't believe. They don't live here. But *we* know," Kim says.

I don't know what Việt Kiều means, but I don't like Kim just putting that label on me. She doesn't know me or what I believe.

"How do you break the curse?" Anne asks.

Kim shrugs. "In some houses, their curses were broken." She points to two houses beyond the play structure. "I don't know how, but my uncle said they were broken by the people in the families."

"Like us?" I ask.

"No. Not you," Not-Happy Guy, Vinh says.

"Hey, we're Vietnamese like you," Anne says.

"No." Vinh looks at me and my siblings. "You're

not like us. Go back to your own country!" He kicks the ball down the field, and Kim runs after it. The rest of the kids go back to the game too.

It's like I've been punched in the stomach. We don't say anything as we walk back to the house with our heads down.

As soon as we get there, I go to the backyard to practice Taekwondo. My Make-New-Friends-in-Town Plan has failed. And I'm soooo mad, I could just scream. How dare Vinh make me feel less than them, make me feel I'm not Vietnamese enough. Dad says this is our homeland. But is it?

As Anne helps with dinner and Jay sits at the table waiting (nobody ever expects him to help!), I touch my pearl earrings. I wait for the rushing wind to know Grandma Nội is near. It doesn't happen. Is it because of the curse? I feel icy cold down my back again. Is the house trying to get me to notice something?

For the first time since coming to Vietnam, I feel all alone.

CHAPTER 6: JAY

Not a Great Feeling

We're having dinner, but I'm not the hungry goat I usually am. I tie up my long hair just like Anne does. She has that worried look on her face Liz calls Miss Perfect's Responsible Face.

Trai or gái? That's what the kid at the park said about me. Boy or girl? My sisters don't think I know those words, but I do. I listen in sometimes on their Vietnamese lessons back at home.

I wanted to yell at the kids—*there are more than two choices!* But I don't have the words in Vietnamese. I feel different here—smaller somehow—without the language.

But Vinh is right about something. We're not like those kids. I wonder what it would be like to grow up here, where everyone was born here and speaks the same language and knows about all the same things. Would everyone feel like they belonged? Or would some still feel different? Knowing what it's like to feel different, I know it's not a great feeling.

Anne puts meat in my bowl. She stares at me, almost reading my mind. "Ignore them. There are always mean people," she says.

"I didn't expect it here," Liz replies, getting herself some food.

Cô Ba sits down after setting some cut watermelon on the table. She smiles at me. I hope she's happy we're here.

"Cám ơn," I say, thanking her.

We eat for a bit without anyone talking.

Cô Ba points to the watermelon. "Your Nội. My mom. Love!" Then points to her mouth and smiles widely. "I love."

We all smile, and my shoulders feel more relaxed.

"Cô Ba, do you have stories of our Grandma Nội?" Anne asks when we're almost done dinner.

"Bà Nội. Live here. Đây," Liz says.

Cô Ba gets up and points to a chest under the stairs.

"Bà Nội's stuff?" I ask as we all come over.

"Wow," I say, ready to pounce like a tiger as she opens it.

The chest smells like Grandma Nội—medicine oil, tea, and fried treats from the kitchen. The smell makes me so sad and happy, remembering her and missing her at the same time.

The chest is packed with her photo albums, stacks of fabric, books, and notebooks. Cô Ba picks up a metal tool that looks the same as what Mom has for pressing potatoes through little holes for making mashed potatoes.

"Bánh lọt. Dessert," Cô Ba said. "Your Nội. My mom. Bad." She squeezes the tool together and then shakes her head. She bursts out laughing.

My auntie has a big laugh that sounds the same as Grandma Nội's.

"I guess when the sisters made dessert using this tool, it was a disaster!" Liz laughs too.

I see a wooden box at the bottom. "What's this?"

Cô Ba nods, so I open it carefully. Inside, there's a paintbrush with a dark wooden handle and soft hairs.

Cô Ba reaches over and takes the paintbrush gently out of the box.

She starts waving it around in big, swooping swirls. She points at my fan in the back pocket of my shorts.

I reach behind and open my fan, revealing all the painted animals of the zodiac.

"Grandma Nội told me her dad painted the animals on here," I say.

"That must be his brush!" Liz says in an excited voice.

Grandma's dad's brush . . . that's so cool! I think of Grandma Nội and wonder if she's here.

As everyone is looking through a photo album, I turn around. I do what I've done at home to be close to her. I trace the rat on my fan. No glitter.

I trace all the animals, but nothing happens. I can't connect to Grandma Nội.

The snowstorm is back in my head, jumbling everything together, just like yesterday. It feels like the house is doing that, causing the snowstorm. Is the house trying to tell me something about Grandma and about the curse?

I'm not going to tell Anne or Liz about the fan. They'll think I'm a baby and can't do stuff. I breathe in and out, feeling alone.

CHAPTER 7: ANNE
Clues

I wake up suddenly, completely covered in sweat.

As I turn over in bed, I can't stop thinking about what Vinh said yesterday. *No, you're not like us.* And the ugly look he gave us, as if he was smelling something bad.

When Dad told us we were going to Vietnam, I was super excited to learn about my culture and my identity. I did a lot of research. I have it all organized into files on the laptop, just the way I like. Coming here, it's cool to see people who look like me. But now I realize that's not everything. I am still different.

I check the tablet. 5:43 a.m. Sunday morning.

I see Liz is still sleeping so I slip down to the kitchen. I'm surprised to see Cô Ba there already. She has a bunch of ingredients in bowls—one is a green paste—and a little pot on the stove.

"Morning! Help?" I ask.

She nods and hands me a whisk. "Make bánh lọt."

We add the ingredients to the pot, and I stir the whole time as it heats up. When it's pretty thick, Cô Ba spoons some of the batter into the tool we found in Grandma Nội's chest. Then she squeezes it through into a bowl of ice water. It comes out looking like green wormies!

She hands the tool to me. I do it too, giggling as I imagine Grandma Nội and her sister doing this exact thing. Maybe doing this reminds Cô Ba of her mom too.

Cô Ba puts some in a bowl with sugar water and coconut milk. Together, we try the bánh lọt. It's delicious!

I grab pen and paper and quickly write down the recipe, reading some of the ingredients from their container labels. Cooking with Cô Ba is like cooking with Grandma Nội, helping me connect to my Vietnamese-ness.

I write a note to myself: *super awesome with maple syrup?* I put the recipe near my laptop in the living room.

As Cô Ba cleans up, I make three bowls of bánh lọt and head back upstairs to the ancestors' room. I set out the offerings like I do at home. I sit on the mat in front of the altar.

"Anne?"

I hear Jay and Liz walking downstairs. Still in their pajamas, they sit down on either side of me.

"Couldn't sleep?" I ask.

Jay rests his head on my shoulder, and Liz puts her head in my lap as we sit on the mat.

"The house woke me up. My head feels fuzzy," Jay says.

"Cold. The house feels sooo chilly. When it's so hot in Vietnam," Liz adds.

"I get a heaviness from the house. Like there's something sitting right on top of me," I reply.

We sit quietly for a few minutes.

Then Jay whispers, "Don't laugh. I think the house is trying to tell us something. About the curse."

"At the park, Kim said the house is cursed because Grandma Nội never came back to it after she left for Canada. She said none of the ancestors can come back now," Liz adds.

"Why didn't Grandma ever come back?" Jay asks.

"Maybe it would be too sad for her." I shrug. "But I know I can't feel her here."

"Me either. Do you think her spirit wants to come back but can't?" Jay asks.

I put my head in my hands, feeling the sense of heaviness come over me again, right across my shoulders, weighing me down.

"We have to break the curse for her spirit to be able to return!" Liz is getting excited now. I can tell she is starting to form one of her plans.

I notice my jade bangle is changing colors. It feels different than when Grandma visits me at home, but it does seem like it's trying to tell me something.

Two years ago, Grandma Nội asked me to help her cook Vietnamese food because the ancestors were not happy. Is Grandma asking for help now?

My bangle begins to glow with a rainbow of colors. I can't look away, but I don't think Jay and Liz notice.

"Kim said those other families had to break the curse," Jay says.

Just as Jay says that, the glowing gets brighter. Jay is right! The house is giving us clues. And it's happening through my bangle! The house is telling us that we are family, and the house wants us here!

"It's up to us as her grandkids to help her," I say, feeling this is something I have to do.

CHAPTER 8: LIZ
I'll Be the Star

Miss Perfect may actually be right about some-thing. We need to help Grandma. I have a new plan, the Break-the-Curse Plan. I skip down to the living room.

"Đi?" Cô Ba asks me and points out the door, interrupting my planning.

I leap over to her. I love being around her.

My new auntie. She's so nice! Before we leave the house, I give her the friendship bracelet I made for her. I made it out of yellow and orange and green thread because that's how I think of her, warm and sunny and active!

"Đẹp quá," she says as she holds it between her fingers.

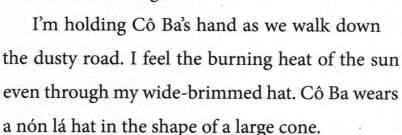

I tie it around her wrist. She smiles and hugs me.

I'm holding Cô Ba's hand as we walk down the dusty road. I feel the burning heat of the sun even through my wide-brimmed hat. Cô Ba wears a nón lá hat in the shape of a large cone.

There's really no sidewalk, so I hop over holes and bits of trash. Moving around helps me think.

It keeps my body strong, and my mind. Auntie Hai told me I'm the daughter of strong Vietnamese women, like the Trung Warriors.

A man and woman on a motorbike, close to auntie's age, zoom up beside us and stop.

"Đây là ai?" The man asks my auntie who I am. His voice is loud and sharp.

Cô Ba and the couple talk in Vietnamese. I don't know all the words. I watch though. At first, auntie seems surprised, then nervous, her voice shaking. She squeezes my hand. Possibly many neighbors don't talk to her. I remember the unfriendly kids. *You live in one of those houses*, Kim said. Do the neighbors not like Cô Ba because the house is cursed? That's sooo not fair! It's not her fault Grandma Nội didn't want to come back. Don't be mean to her!

The couple just stare at me, which happens a lot in Vietnam.

I wave and smile. If they see how nice I am, hopefully they will be nicer to Cô Ba. "Hello. Xin chào!" I say and nod my head in polite greeting.

The woman suddenly smiles, and they all keep talking. The tone of the neighbors' voices is gentler now. Cô Ba starts to relax, her shoulders loosen, and her breathing is more normal. She smiles too and then rests both her hands on my shoulders. "Cháu gái ngoan. Về thăm nhà."

"You come home. You good!" The man gives me a thumbs-up before they drive off.

As we get close to home, Cô Ba says, "Nhà quên."

The house forgot.

I look at Cô Ba, and there is a look in her eyes . . . hope. What does she hope for? I get an icy chill down my back again. I touch my earrings. I'm not sure why, but they begin to hum in a low tone. Is that the sound of crying? Tears. Saying goodbye. People leaving and people staying.

I realize my Break-the-Curse Plan is not just for Grandma Nội. But for Cô Ba too. For those who left and those still here. I feel even more sure now that if the house forgot, then the house could remember! The sounds I hear from my earrings change to a gentle laughing. Does the house like my plan now that it's starting to know us? Is that

Cô Ba's hope? That me and Anne and Jay could help the house remember?

"Nhà nhớ?" I ask and hug her.

Cô Ba is smiling, more than I've ever seen before. I think she wants the curse to be broken. For Grandma and for all the ancestors to be able to come home.

And when I break the curse, I'll show those kids from yesterday. I'm just as Vietnamese as they are. I'll be the star.

I run back to the kitchen to tell Jay and Anne what just happened. I stop.

Miss Perfect and The Baby are at the table.

Jay says something as he packs up great-grandpa's paintbrush. Anne bursts out laughing.

My brother never tries to make me laugh like that. Anne hugs him. Jay smiles. My sister never takes care of me like that.

They seem so happy. I'm the outsider. Again. I hate feeling this way!

They don't need me. So I don't need them.

I won't tell them. I'll finish the Break-the-Curse Plan myself. I run up the stairs to the ancestors' room.

CHAPTER 9: JAY
Strong Like a Dragon

As Anne sets out lunch, she seems worried. So I tell her a fart joke, and she laughs so hard. It's not really my thing, but everyone laughs at fart jokes.

"Get Liz, please. Cô Ba is here. Lunch is ready," Anne says as she sets out chopsticks.

I make sure my painting is dry before closing my sketchbook.

Cô Ba sets down rice paper and grilled meat.

Hugging my sketchbook tight, I walk to the backyard, but my sister isn't there.

"Liz?" I call out.

Where could she be? Didn't she just come in with Cô Ba? She's not on the main level so I head up the stairs, swinging up the railing like a monkey.

I find her in the room of ancestors.

"Hey, why are you here alone?" I say to her.

Liz doesn't say anything.

She's unhappy. I can tell because when she's like that, she leans her body away from everyone.

I try again as I walk over to her.

"Did you have a nice walk with Cô Ba?"

Liz is sitting at the table, flipping through a photo album. They are really old photos, black and white, of people I don't know.

"Do you want to see my new painting?" I open my sketchbook. "I did it when you were out. I used Grandma Nội's dad's paintbrush."

"It's of this house," we both say at the same time.

It felt so cool picking up the brush and dipping it in paint. I use pencil most of the time. The feeling of making brushstrokes is so different, more free. I felt like a snake sliding my arm across the heavy paper.

"Grandma Nội used to put her hands on my shoulders when I drew," I

say as I lay my painted fan next to the painting of the house.

"You did great," Liz whispers. It looks like she's going to cry. But at least she's talking to me now.

The blizzard starts again in my mind. Beside the painting of the house, my fan is sparkling in the sunlight.

Back at home, the fan has helped me by showing me how I can be myself in so many different ways, like the different animals. I wonder . . . is it trying to help me now? Is it showing me something about the house?

I look at my painting again. I think of the people who lived here and didn't come back. Now I want to cry too.

Suddenly, on my fan, all the animals seem to disappear, as if they've been erased.

I hold my breath, and my heart begins to race. Is the house doing this to my fan? Is it telling me about the people who lived here and left?

Slowly, one by one, the animals shimmer back into place. I wonder . . . is the house telling me we're also part of the family who lived here?

Like the animals reappearing on the fan, we're

here in the house now. Is the house trying to get to know us?

"Jay? Liz? Hello! Lunch!" Anne calls out. She comes into the room, looks at us, and walks over to the table. "What's going on?"

We must both look very sad.

I move closer to my sisters, wanting us to stick together like a herd of buffalo. I miss Dad and Mom. But it's only Sunday, and they're not back until Wednesday. I wipe away my tears quickly, so my sisters don't see. I try to be strong like a dragon.

CHAPTER 10: ANNE
So I Am Different?

"Where are we?" I ask my uncle, Chú Tư. He's my dad's other cousin, Cô Ba's brother. He's the reason we're here, standing in this super-long line.

"Núi Bà Đen," he replies. "Black Lady Mountain."

"Isn't this place cool?" Liz says out loud but avoids looking at me. I think she's still mad from yesterday.

"Very famous. There's a legend that a brave girl died on the mountain. Her spirit is still here. People built a temple in her honor. We'll ride the gondola to the top," he replies.

We had to get up really early to be here. Cô Ba stands a few people behind us. In between are a bunch of cousins and second cousins . . . I think. It feels super strange that I'm meeting them all for the first time.

"I'm Linh. We're cousins," a girl says to us and takes Liz's hand.

I smile. "Hi, Linh."

I wish I had more time to get to know everyone.

I hear Vietnamese all around me, like music, with all the melodic tones. There are so many

black-haired people here. Most stare at me. Am I one of them?

Even though things are not great at home with my two best friends, Jennifer and Sophie, it's not great here either. I thought being in Vietnam would make me MORE SURE about who I am, not less sure.

"Việt Kiều," I hear someone whisper as they pass by.

"Chú Tư, what does Việt Kiều mean?" I ask.

He laughs but then shakes his head. "Overseas Vietnamese."

"Me?" I say.

He nods.

"How do people know?" I ask.

He shrugs. "Your style. Your look. It's different."

"So I am different?" I ask, an emptiness in my stomach.

"We are all different from each other. And we are all alike—Vietnamese." He slings an arm over my shoulders. "Cô Ba said she was happy you made bánh lọt with her. I'm glad you're here, to know your country. To know yourself."

Out of nowhere, I remember a couple years ago when I was cooking chả giò with Grandma Nội. I said I didn't know who I am, and she told me that I am Anne Nguyen and that all the ancestors are in me. My heart glows thinking about this now.

I may not feel the rushing wind and Grandma's

presence, but cooking with Cô Ba did make me feel closer to Grandma Nội. I'm even more determined to help her. Yesterday, I tried to look up "how to break a curse" on my laptop, but the Internet was so glitchy. If I don't break it before we have to leave, Grandma might be stuck forever! Breaking it will prove I belong in Vietnam.

The line finally starts to move. Liz, just ahead of me, seems to be having a great time with Linh and our other cousins.

But Jay is standing alone looking down. He must still be sad from yesterday.

I walk past Liz over to him. Liz gives me a funny look, but I smile at her.

I put my arms around Jay.

"I want to go home," he says.

I can't think of any fart jokes to tell him.

Liz comes over to us. "Aww, Miss Perfect and The Baby . . . soooo sweet!"

Jay throws my arm off. He *hates* being called the baby.

Yikes! Why is Liz picking a fight? And in front of our family?

"Stop!" Jay shouts. He pushes Liz, who stumbles backward a bit. People start to stare.

My cheeks feel hot. This is super embarrassing.

CHAPTER 11: LIZ

Not All This Other Stuff about Feelings!

"You stop," I say, pushing Jay back. My ears get hot.

When Miss Perfect put her arm around The Baby just now, I saw red inside my head. So jealous!

"Both of you, stop!" Anne says.

"You're not the boss!" I yell.

"You're not Mom!" Jay says at the same time.

I look at Anne. "You don't include me! Not at home and not here!" I shout. All the bad feelings I've been holding inside rush out of me like a burst water balloon.

Coming to Vietnam was a BIG mistake. At home, I have my friends. And my coding. And I'm looking forward to Taekwondo competitions this fall.

I just wanted to come to Vietnam to eat junk food. Make new friends. Have fun. Not all this other stuff about feelings!

"You make me feel like I don't belong in the family!" I remember what Vinh said before to us. "As if I'm not like you both."

Anne shakes her head, hurt. "It's you who doesn't think of me! Of us!"

"Just stop fighting," Jay whispers.

"What?" I yell.

"You shut us out. You're the one who doesn't include us," Anne says.

No one says anything. The rest of the family take a step away, not sure what to do. Cô Ba has already gone up on a gondola.

"Why didn't you help us set out lunch yesterday?" Jay asks me. "Why were you all alone in the room of ancestors?"

I don't want to tell them I ran away from them. I cross both arms in front of me. "I want to help Grandma and break the curse," I say instead.

"Kids, the gondola is coming," Chú Tư says quietly. "Can you get along, please?"

"Yes, Uncle, sorry," Anne says. Her cheeks are pink.

I mutter I'm sorry too.

As I sit in the large gondola, it's like someone punched me. Is that what I do, not include them?

I play with the friendship bracelets on my wrist. I made them hoping to give them away today to family members. Looking around, I'm surrounded by family who want to get to know me. I realize I *have* had a ton of fun here in Vietnam. Surrounded by people who love me.

And all my anger leaves quickly like water down a drain.

When we get to the top of the mountain, I see a beautiful statue of a lady wearing black. She looks brave and calm. She reminds me of the Trung Warriors.

I stand beside Anne. Looking at the statue, I find the courage to be the first to reach out.

I squeeze her hand. "I thought of something when I was walking with Cô Ba yesterday. To break the curse, we need to help the house remember."

"Remember what?" Anne asks.

Jay, who had come up behind us, says, "Family. Us staying at the house is already helping the house remember. The house is starting to know us." He breathes out and takes my other hand. "We can do it. We can break the curse, all the way."

Anne sighs. "Liz, you don't have to do it by yourself. Grandma Nội needs *all* of us."

We look at each other and smile.

Later on, the sun is setting, and it's the most

beautiful color of deepest red. My cousin Linh walks with me back to the gondola ride, her arm through mine. She's sooooo nice, I'm happy to now know her. I'll make a friendship bracelet especially for her.

Linh asks, "You okay?"

I nod and smile. "I am."

CHAPTER 12: JAY
I Know What We Need

After breakfast on Tuesday, I video chat with Grandpa Nội. Finally! He's getting ready for bed back at home.

"Grandpa, khỏe không?" I ask Grandpa how he's doing.

He gives me a thumbs-up. "You?" he asks.

I'm in the room of ancestors. I want to talk

about the curse. But Grandpa's English is not great. And my Vietnamese sucks.

"Grandpa, look," I say, holding up the painting I did of the house. "You like?"

Grandpa nods, saying, "Tốt quá." It's so good.

I hold up Grandma Nội's dad's paintbrush. "I used this." I wave the paintbrush around my painted fan.

He freezes on the screen. No, don't be glitchy now.

He smiles and claps his hands. "Family paintbrush. You same as great-grandpa. Great-grandpa same as you."

"Thanks, Grandpa." I smile. I am like my great-grandpa. I look over at the framed pictures of my ancestors. I think of my family. My great-grandpa, Grandma Nội, Dad, me. All of us, connected.

For the first time since being in Vietnam, I feel like I could be part of this place. Sure, Vinh is mean. But Cô Ba and Chú Tư and Linh and my other cousins are all nice and welcoming. Maybe Vietnam isn't so bad. I can be myself here. I could try.

I take the brush, and almost without thinking, trace over my painting of the house, feeling all the strokes again.

I think about Grandma Nội's dad using this brush to paint the animals. I wonder . . . I then trace over all the animals with his brush.

For the first time since coming to this house, I feel a little breeze. It's warm and comforting.

Grandma Nội, is that you?

"Grandma's fan! Back. First time," Grandpa says as he sees me holding it up.

The painted fan. Grandma Nội's gift. Back in the house! Is that why I can start to feel her again, on the wind? Is the house starting to remember her, through the fan? The blizzard in my mind starts to clear and I feel calm.

"Bracelet. Earrings. Fan. First time all back," Grandpa Nội says.

I nod and think of the house as having cracks in it when it forgot. Now that Grandma's gifts are here and we are here, the cracks are starting to mend, starting to heal.

I wish Grandpa a good night and end the call.

"Anne! Liz!" I yell.

Anne comes upstairs. "Yes?"

"I have something to tell you. Where's Liz?"

"Here." Liz walks in. "I went for a bike ride."

"I know what we need to break the curse completely." I catch my breath. I hold up my painted fan. I point at Anne's wrist and Liz's ear.

"What?" Anne asks, holding up her bangle.

"How do you know?" Liz asks, touching her earrings.

"I just know. And the house knows! Grandma knows," I respond. "If what Dad says is right, this

is our homeland. That's why it must be us who break the curse." I'm an excited rooster, using my voice.

"Because we're part of the family who is here?" Liz asks.

"And we've brought back Grandma's gifts," I add. "It's the first time they've come back to the house since Grandma Nội left. Grandpa told me."

"If the house is remembering, the gifts could help," Anne says, nodding her head.

"Mom and Dad come back tomorrow. Then we leave this house!" I yell. "We must do it now!"

"But what do we do with the gifts?" Liz asks.

None of us has an answer.

CHAPTER 13: ANNE

Our Ancestors Who Came before Me

My heart is beating super fast and it's hard to think.

I am in the ancestors' room, pacing. Jay is standing nearby. Liz is sitting on the table swinging her legs. They are both waiting. Waiting for me to come up with a plan. I feel their eyes on my back and the heaviness on my shoulders. This time, it's too much pressure, almost pushing me down with the weight. My hands are so sweaty.

I touch my jade bangle. *Grandma Nội, what do I do?*

Nothing happens. No rushing wind.

"Aargh!" I scream. I take off my jade bangle. I'm so annoyed!

My eyes fall on the altar. It's super weird that there's so much empty space. Usually, we place flowers or food and drink on the altar. As an offering to the ancestors. Wait. An offering . . .

"Anne?" Jay asks.

"Let me try something." I place my jade bangle on the altar.

Jay looks at me then looks at the altar. He puts

his painted fan next to my jade bangle.

"Will this work?" Liz asks as she takes off her pearl earrings and adds them to the altar.

Please, let this work.

Nothing happens.

"Why won't this work? Grandma Nội left. She didn't visit. Now we are here. We are part of the family who lived in this house. And we are offering gifts from Grandma Nội." I start pacing. "Why is that not enough?"

Liz says, "No, that isn't enough!"

"Not helpful, Liz!" I yell.

"Don't fight," Jay whispers.

"I mean, we need more," Liz says. "What about our own gifts? Something to the ancestors from us?"

"Like what?" I ask.

Liz takes off one of her friendship bracelets. It's red and yellow thread woven together. She's been making those the whole trip and giving them away to family. She lays it on the altar too.

"Jay, do you have something?" she asks.

Jay takes something off the table. "I do." He places his painting of the house on the altar.

The hairs on my arm stand up as I notice my siblings' actions.

I understand something.

I do not always have to take care of everything. I do not always have to be the strong one and be so lonely. I am the oldest, but my sister and brother are super smart and capable too. I feel the heaviness lifting off me. They lean on me, but I can lean on them too.

"Anne—" Liz begins.

"Great idea, Liz!" I say. I get the recipe for bánh lọt from my backpack. I lay it on the altar too.

As soon as I do, all the objects begin to glow softly, the colors of a sunrise. These are all things we created while here in Vietnam, in this house.

"It's working," I say. I feel a gentle breeze.

"We need incense. We always need incense to talk to Grandma Nội," Jay says.

"You're right," I reply. I take out joss sticks, light them quickly, and hand them out.

Grandma Nội told me about our ancestors who came before me, and I think of them, known and unknown, surrounding us, hugging us. A warmth comes over me from the top of my head and down through my body.

CHAPTER 14: LIZ

Is It Working?

I can feel both Anne and Jay breathing. I feel silly now being jealous when we were at the mountain yesterday. Both my sister and my brother are here with me. Together, we can do anything.

"Think of Grandma Nội!" Anne says.

I try to think of her. Her hands along my cheeks. Her stories of the Trung Warriors.

I look up at the ancestors' altar and I look at Grandma Nội's gifts. They all came from here. Fan. Wood from the trees. Bangle. Jade from the earth. Earrings. Pearls from the sea. They are also part of our daily life at home. Jay dances around with his fan. Anne wears her bangle making food. I always wear my earrings at Taekwondo.

Then I look at our gifts. Discovering the house. Offering food. Making friendships. We ARE connected to Vietnam too.

All the gifts are glowing. All the gifts are needed to break the curse. They all belong. If I'm also needed, then does that mean I belong too?

I notice that the smoke from the incense is making its way to the ceiling.

"Let me try something. Grandma Nội helped me know who I am," my sister says beside me. "I am Anne Nguyen."

"I am Jay Nguyen," Jay says.

"Good idea!" I say. Yes, we need a spell. "I am Liz Nguyen."

The gifts start to grow brighter and brighter.

"I think it's working!" I shout.

Both my siblings close their eyes. I shut mine too. We wait.

There is a blinding light that I can see even with my eyes closed.

Then a loud BOOM! My ears start to ring.

Then . . . the rushing wind!

"Grandma Nội!" Jay says.

I open my eyes.

You did it, you broke the curse! The house remembers our family now. And I can come home!

I hear a voice on the wind. Grandma Nội is close by. The air smells clean and fresh. I feel a warm breeze, a warm hug.

"Grandma, we missed you," Anne says.

I'm always here. The curse on the house was made after people like me left Vietnam and didn't come back.

"Grandma Nội, why didn't you visit this house?" I ask.

It was hard to leave the first time. It would be too painful to come back and have to leave again. Only you kids could break the curse!

"Why us?" Anne asks.

You came here looking for a connection to this land, looking for something of yourselves in Vietnam. Did you find what you were looking for?

I nod. I think my siblings nod too.

"We belong," Jay whispers.

Vietnam is always a part of you. All the ancestors are in you.

"Your gifts helped," I say, and then realize, "and we found our own gifts here too."

Grandchildren, you have to know. YOU are the gifts.

Tears begin to roll down my cheeks.

You are free to make your own way in the world. Be who you are. I love who you are.

Her words are carried on the wind. I pull Anne and Jay into a tight hug.

"I'm glad we came to Vietnam," Anne says, tears shining in her eyes. She stands up straighter, like she put down her invisible backpack.

"Me too. Even with all this feelings stuff!" I add, and we all laugh.

For the first time, I notice Cô Ba by the door. She enters the room, which she hasn't done before. We pull her into our hug.

CHAPTER 15: JAY

Be Who I Am

It's finally Wednesday, the day Dad and Mom are coming back! Cô Ba is throwing a big party to celebrate the return of the ancestors. Family and neighbors are all around. People smile and call me Jay and want to hug me. I'm a dog the whole family loves. I show people my drawings of the house and they all clap.

My sisters and I agreed we'll leave our offerings here in Vietnam. My painting. Liz's friendship bracelet. Anne's recipe. They belong in the house, to represent us and our connection here. And a promise to come back. I think Grandma Nội is happy with our decision.

A bunch of kids are in the kitchen. Linh and Liz are eating Anne's chả giò spring rolls. We already laid out some rolls on Grandma Nội's newly cleaned altar.

Kim stands up. "Sorry, I have to go. Come play soccer with us later."

"Not if Vinh's there," Liz says right away.

"He feels bad for what he said. When his cousins from California visit here, they tease him.

Say he's not like them. Please come," Kim says and turns to go.

"I always wanted to live somewhere else, like California," Linh replies, eating another roll.

"And I wonder what it's like living here," Liz replies, playing with her pearl earrings.

"I hope you'll come back again, to visit your homeland." Linh hugs Liz and then hugs me.

"You could travel to see us too," I add.

"They're back!" Anne shouts from the living room.

"Dad! Mom!" I yell and run to the front of the house, holding my painted fan.

They get out of the taxi.

"Jay! Buddy!" Dad says.

Dad hugs me, and I'm a dragon—I could fly! I let out a long breath. He goes to hug my sisters as I hug Mom.

Cô Ba comes up behind us and says something in Vietnamese.

Other people come to greet my parents.

"How was your trip?" Anne asks.

"Lovely!" Mom replies.

"So lovely I don't know how we'll pay for it all once we're back home," Dad says, laughing, but a bit nervous too.

Mom gives Dad *a look*. Then she turns to us. "So how was it here?" she asks, her voice lighter.

My siblings and I look at each other. We share silly smiles.

Liz can't hold back anymore. "Grandma Nội's spirit and the spirits of all the ancestors couldn't return to the house. Last night, we broke the curse! We're superstars!"

"We did it with the help of Grandma Nội's gifts," Anne adds, holding up her jade bangle.

"And our own gifts," I say.

Mom smiles.

"That all sounds great!" Dad says, a little distracted, waving to people in the house. "So you've had a good time then?"

We all nod.

Cô Ba hugs Liz from behind, laughing. In this house where my grandma grew up, in this town she called home, where family and friends are now, I laugh too.

The blizzard in my mind is gone. I want to gallop holding my fan, like the happy horse I am. Grandma Nội said Vietnam is always a part of me. And I am free to figure out how being Vietnamese fits with who I am. I can't wait to tell Grandpa everything when we get home.

"When can we come back to Vietnam?" I ask.

Dear diary,

I love bánh tráng rice paper! It is super tasty! We had it for lunch with pork that Cô Ba grilled then drizzled onion oil and peanuts on top. We had to wet the circle of rice paper in hot water until it was soft, sort of like a thin pancake that is sticky and a bit salty. Then we added lettuce, herbs, pickled veggies, rice noodles, and meat, and wrapped the whole thing up like a spring roll and dipped it in fish sauce. It was like eating an entire buffet meal in one bite! No one, not Grandma Nội or my parents, ever showed me this. Super excited to make it at home!

-Anne

Dear Grandpa Nội,

I don't know if I'll send this letter. Or if it's too much English for you. But I want to write it. I miss you. Our chats. The snacks you make. When you hug me and the blizzard in my mind stops.

I have a lot of drawings to show you. There's this one of all the cars and bikes and motorbikes on the road, moving like a river. And one drawing of a water buffalo in a field, thinking about life, open blue sky all around. Vietnam is pretty nice.

See you in a few days. Go Jets go!

Jay

Liz & Linh's Chat

Liz: What's your fave colors?

Linh: Pink and purple

Linh: why?

Liz: Surprise! 🎁

Linh: Keke

Liz: Soooo fun at the mountain today!

Linh: 😊

Liz: We were so high up. Could see clouds and birds and trees.

Liz: Love hanging out!

Liz: Cousin!

Linh: Gift for you too. You like paper stars?

Liz: Love stars! Love gifts!!!!

Liz & Rohan's Chat

Liz: Best Friend Ever, what's for breakfast?

Rohan: Cereal

Liz: Boring!

Rohan: You?

Liz: Going to bed soon. Visited a cool mountain today.

Liz: Hung out with more family.

Rohan: So much family!

Liz: Totally. So fun!

Liz: Need to make more friendship bracelets!

Rohan: Mine?

Liz: Surprise! 🎁

Liz: Miss me?

Rohan: New superhero movie when you're back?

Liz: Love it!

Author's Note

Thanks so much for spending time with Anne, Liz, and Jay in Vietnam. I was three years old when I moved away from Vietnam. I was nine years old when I visited for the first time since leaving. The trip was both puzzling and amazing. So, for this story, I wanted to explore how it may feel to visit a place that is both familiar and strange—feeling like you belong and like you don't belong at the same time. And how the siblings experience things differently. This is my offering.

Having altars to the ancestors is a Vietnamese custom I grew up with after my dad passed away when I was seven years old. We made offerings of food and recognized death anniversaries. You may have your own special ways to remember loved ones.

A note about the language in this series: sometimes the Vietnamese words are spelled in Vietnamese with accents, and they are pronounced in Vietnamese. And sometimes the Vietnamese words have no accents and are pronounced in a way that fits with how words are pronounced in English. I've made these choices based on how I imagine the character would say them/think of them.

For example, Nguyen as a last name is written as Nguyễn in Vietnamese. I have chosen to write it as Nguyen without the accents as I imagine the siblings would write it like that at school and pronounce their last name in an English way.

Also, sometimes I have chosen to merge English and Vietnamese words. In Vietnamese, a person would call their dad's mom Bà Nội and their dad's dad Ông Nội. I have merged Grandma and Grandpa with Nội. A person would call their dad's oldest sister Cô Hai and call their dad's oldest sister's husband Dượng Hai. I merged Auntie and Uncle with Hai. I imagine this is a decision the Nguyen family made. It may be different with each family.

I'm so honored you chose this book. Feel free to reach out to me at lindaytrinh.com. Take care!

Linda

Acknowledgments

As I was writing the third book in the series, *The Mystery of the Painted Fan*, I had the idea for this book—a family trip to Vietnam from rotating points of view. My sense for the book was so strong and compelling that I brought the idea to Annick Press. I'm forever grateful to the entire team for believing in and supporting yet another book in The Nguyen Kids series, *The Journey of the Ancestors' Gifts*. Thanks to Katie for being such a careful and responsive editor. Thanks to Jieun for her perceptive editorial feedback and kind support. Thanks to Eleanor and Mary Ann for their insights. Thanks to Clayton for his amazing illustrations.

Love to all my extended family and friends for their support and thanks to those who read various drafts. Shout out to Jane, Jonathan, Luke, and Anna for our fried chicken dinners and chats. Thanks to John and Leah for workshopping some tricky parts of this book.

Deepest appreciation to my writerly friends. Thanks to my best friend Mirna for our long conversations about young readers and for always being there for me. Thanks to my cousins Ky and Bao for their perspectives and encouragement. Thanks to cousin Liem for his creative point of view. Thanks to my big sister Jen, my biggest fangirl, for loving all my words and helping me explore our Vietnamese heritage. Thanks to my husband Ryan for giving me the space and support to take the chance on myself to be an author.

Thanks to my kids, Lexi and Evan, who inspire me with their curiosity, bravery, kindness, and perseverance. Lexi was my first reader and offered great insights and Evan had great ideas for me. I'm so humbled that they're able to see kids like themselves in this series. Mama loves you! And of course, thanks to my mom, for making this life possible for me, for showing me every day what hard work looked like when I was growing up.

I'll be forever grateful to my dad, my grandparents, and to all my ancestors, for everything they have sacrificed and accomplished so that I may pursue my dreams!

Follow Nguyen siblings Anne, Liz, and Jay on all their adventures as they unlock the secrets of their magical gifts. Collect the whole series, available now!

Also available as e-books and audiobooks.

The Secret of the
JADE BANGLE

ISBN 978-1-77321-715-4 HC
ISBN 978-1-77321-716-1 PB

Anne, the oldest sibling, misses her Grandma Nội a lot. But Grandma's gift to her holds a special power that helps Anne realize no matter how difficult things get, the love of her ancestors is always with her.

The Power of the
PEARL EARRINGS

ISBN 978-1-77321-710-9 HC
ISBN 978-1-77321-711-6 PB

Liz, the middle kid, is determined to prove to everyone that she's just as important and brave as the fierce Trung Sisters, freedom fighters in ancient Vietnam.

The Mystery of the
PAINTED FAN

ISBN 978-1-77321-771-0 HC
ISBN 978-1-77321-772-7 PB

Being the youngest can be tough. But Jacob wants to be true to himself—even when that means many different things at once.

The Journey of the
ANCESTORS' GIFTS

978-1-77321-812-0 HC
978-1-77321-813-7 PB

The siblings are visiting Vietnam for the first time! The moment they arrive at Grandma Nội's old house, though, something is not right—why can't they sense Grandma's spirit?

About the Author

©Kalla Photography

Linda Trinh is a Vietnamese Canadian author who writes stories for kids and grown-ups. Linda moved away from Vietnam when she was three years old and visited for the first time when she was nine years old. On that trip, she got to know her grandparents, aunts, uncles, and cousins and stayed in the house her grandmother grew up in. She toured some of the countryside, learned more Vietnamese, and ate a lot of phở and bánh mì. She spends a lot of time staring out her window, daydreaming, and pacing around the house, writing in her head way before she types out anything. She lives with her husband and two kids in Winnipeg.

About the Illustrator

Clayton Nguyen is an artist working on animated TV shows and films to bring imaginary characters and worlds to life. In a complete coincidence, Clayton also started drawing at an early age and has two older sisters, just like Jacob. Being the youngest sibling, he is still sometimes treated like the baby of the family. Some of his earliest memories of becoming interested in art come from watching TV shows like *Art Attack* and anime with his sisters after school. Nowadays, when he isn't drawing, you'll often find him playing video games or getting bubble tea in Toronto.